The Warm Glow of Happy Homes

ANDERSEN PRUNTY

GRINDHOUSE PRESS

Published by Grindhouse Press
POB 292644
Dayton, OH 45429
www.grindhousepress.com

The Warm Glow of Happy Homes
Grindhouse Press #015
ISBN-13: 978-0-9883484-1-7
ISBN-10: 0988348411

This book is a work of fiction.

Also by Andersen Prunty

Bury the Children in the Yard: Horror Stories

Satanic Summer

Fill the Grand Canyon and Live Forever

Pray You Die Alone: Horror Stories

Sunruined: Horror Stories

The Driver's Guide to Hitting Pedestrians

Hi I'm a Social Disease: Horror Stories

Fuckness

The Sorrow King

Slag Attack

My Fake War

Morning is Dead

The Beard

Zerostrata

Jack and Mr. Grin

The Overwhelming Urge

THE
WARM
GLOW
OF
HAPPY
HOMES

1.

"I'm not a thief, Alex."

Joe sat on the couch looking trapped by Alex's proposition. Alex's cat, Vonnegut, sat on the coffee table in front of Joe, staring at him with the one eye that worked.

Alex turned his stereo on so his roommate couldn't hear what they were talking about and rolled a joint. The music started, warm and bassy with no words. It made Alex think of taking a subway through the middle of the sun. Cheerful and brain melting.

"I wouldn't say I was either." Alex sat on the soft chair next to the couch and sparked the joint. "Actually, at this point, I'm not willing to say I am or am not anything. For guys like us, things are going to fall apart every five years whether we like it or not. It's out of our control." He held the joint out to Joe. Joe shook his head. "Seriously?"

"I want to be clearheaded to fend off your arguments."

"No arguments. We're having a *rational* discussion."

"Okay, so we're poor, but we're free. As in not in jail. We do something like this and get caught, that changes.

And then we get out of jail and we have a record and then we can't even get jobs as good as we have now."

"I'm telling you, this guy is out of his head. I don't know if it's drugs or brain damage or what but I've been watching him the last three weeks. Ever since that time in the rose garden. It would probably be a month before they even noticed. Nobody's seen the parents since the beginning of summer."

"Yeah yeah. Let me just sit and think about it for a second. You're busy anyway." Joe gestured to the joint currently going to waste between Alex's fingers.

Joe and Alex worked for HappyLawn. Not the best job in the world but they got a lot of rain days off and drew unemployment in the winter. Alex had developed this scheme when they were doing some yard work for the Kings on Lennox Court. He was out weeding in the Kings' rose garden when their son came out. The son lived in the guest house, which was roughly twice the size of most normal houses but about a quarter the size of their main house. He came up to Alex and started yelling about the band the New Kids on the Block, his eyes went blank, and he looked down at the ground and made these clicking sounds. Then he looked up at a nearby tree, screamed, and ran as fast as he could back into the guest house. Alex initially felt like he should be concerned and went to go check on him. He knocked on the door and there wasn't an answer so he turned the knob and it opened. He didn't go inside because they were always told by their superiors that they were invisible, only there to do their jobs, and shouldn't meddle in other people's affairs. This was theory only. Policy. Something to be invoked only when it made their job easier. Most of the guys he worked with, himself included, had fucked at least one of the housewives whose yard work they were supposed to be doing. So he'd watched and listened to the son and, more importantly, had run into the maid at a bar one night and started hanging out with her. She told him about the parents being gone for the summer and that the son was planning some kind of party. There was a safe in the guest house and she knew the combination to it if it was actually locked, which it usually wasn't. She could deactivate the alarm before she left for the day. She knew the code to that too. They could be in and out within a half hour. Easy.

"Come on!" Alex said. "You're always talking about how much you hate the rich shits we work for. You're a smart guy. You probably even have some theory to make it make sense or something."

Joe nodded.

"So come on. That fucker's watch probably costs more than we make in two years."

Joe sighed. "I don't want to do this. I would rather be poor for the rest of my life than go to jail for a month. Besides, it's not like we'll be able to quit working with what we pull out of this spoiled shit's safe. What about cameras?"

"This is the beautiful thing. They have them in the main house but none in the guest house. From what Ibbie says the kid's probably a creep and cameras would just mean evidence in some kind of law suit."

Joe leaned back on the couch and looked at the ceiling.

"This can't just be about money. What's the real reason you want to go through with this? We've been doing this job for years and you've never actually been serious about something like this. Besides, I don't know if I can do it if money is the *only* factor. Is it Ibbie?"

Alex leaned forward and roached the joint in an empty ashtray. He looked at Joe with reddening eyes and said, "Pretty astute."

2.

Barton King stared out one of the large windows in his bedroom studying the way the light fell on a particular section of lawn. He stared for a while but couldn't figure out why until he saw a small portion of the blue sky above the abundant and mature trees in the back yard ripped open and one of those enormous birds fly out. He didn't know what this particular bird was called but he'd seen more and more of them lately. They were always carrying something dangling from their beaks. He didn't know what it was. Something like meat. Since they had to tear the sky open to get here, he assumed they came from space.

He pulled his phone from his pocket to take a picture of the bird but it was already gone so he stripped off his shirt, wandered around the room until he found lighting that made him look really ripped, snapped a few photos of himself, scanned through and scrutinized them until he found the most flattering one, and uploaded it to Facebook.

If Jayne knew what was good for her, she would leave a positive comment within a half hour.

All this activity exhausted Barton and he lay down on

the bed to wait, his head reeling. Sometimes when the room and the house were quiet like this he thought he could hear sheets of paper being ripped in half in a distant room. Maybe one that didn't exist.

The maid came in. Barton had his eyes closed and opened them just long enough to see that it was the young, attractive one, not the huge older one who was probably her mother or something. All those people were related. Barton adjusted his recumbent pose to be more statuesque. He could feel her eyes running all over his body. This thought – the thought of being somebody else with the ability to look at himself from the outside and feel that sense of aesthetic pleasure they must feel – aroused him. He checked Facebook on his phone and thought, *Fuck it. That bitch is never going to comment.* He considered going to his profile and updating it to say they were no longer in a relationship but his penis was painfully straining against his underwear and someone was ripping pages furiously and he thought of a dark and distant planet in space, all of those birds flying around with hunks of flesh or something, and then he heard the shower curtain draw back and the toilet seat being flipped up and he hastily scrawled an entry in his journal his father insisted he keep, even if it wasn't necessarily true.

He wrote: I FELE BRAIN DIED

He slowly rolled out of bed, took a couple of deep breaths, and went to stand in the bathroom doorway.

The maid was bent over the toilet and Barton traced the line of her underwear through her one-piece uniform.

He moved behind her and put his left hand around her

throat.

"You can scream, but there's no one else here," he said. "So don't. Just let me do what I want to do and I'll make it up to you."

He still felt all of her muscles drawn tight against him like she wanted to scream or run or both. He tightened his grip to remind her how fleeting life was and her muscles relaxed somewhat. He put both hands on her shoulders and forced her to her knees. He got on his knees behind her and lifted the hem of her skirt to her waist. He unbuttoned and unzipped his pants and pulled them down with his underwear, freeing his painful erection. He pulled her underwear down and spat in the palm of his hand and rubbed it up and down his penis. Using the excess spit, he put his hand between her buttocks and worked a finger into her anus. He thought she was crying but he couldn't see her face so he couldn't be sure. They would have to make it quick so she could continue putting poison down the drains so the rats wouldn't eat Barton in his sleep. Now he was pretty sure she was crying. He tapped her on the shoulder and said, "Miss, could you please stop crying? It makes me sad."

Maybe she stopped and maybe she didn't. He couldn't really tell. He worked his penis into her ass as far as he could, which wasn't very far. He pushed harder. He worked himself in and out and it got a little easier. Beside the toilet, he noticed the toilet brush she had carelessly laid there. He picked it up, grabbing it midway down the plastic handle. He pressed the handle into her face until she opened her mouth. He forced it into her mouth until she gagged. Every

3.

He went back into the bedroom and checked his phone and noticed Jayne still hadn't commented on his picture. He went to her wall, wrote "BITCH! BITCH! BITCH! BITCH!", went to his profile and severed their connection. He wanted to smash his phone against something. Instead, he threw it savagely against the plush bed and looked down at his shriveling dick. Blood and shit were drying to it. He felt dirty. He hadn't seen the maid leave and didn't want to wash in a dirty shower so he decided to go soak in the pool instead.

He didn't bother putting any swim trunks on.

4.

The sun was disgustingly bright and he wished for like the
millionth time his parents would spring for an indoor pool.
He took off running from the sliding glass doors and leapt
at the edge of the pool, pulling his knees up to his chest and
shouting, "Cannonball!" as he hit the chilly water and let
himself sink to the bottom. When he bobbed to the top a
few minutes later he laughed uproariously and climbed out
of the pool. He squeezed a generous amount of sunblock
into his palms and slathered it all over his body. He looked
at the pool and thought it would be better if it was filled
with dead dogs. He would have tweeted that but his phone
was still in the house and he thought he could see a dead rat
that must have fought its way out of the filter floating on
the other side of the pool and the truth about his image of
the dead dogs was a little too chilling and close to home.
He collapsed into a chair and let the sun dry the moisture
on his body, basking in the sterile scents of the chlorine and
sunblock and the heavily fertilized lawn.

The main house sat closer to the road, way across the

pool and another expanse of immaculate lawn. For a second, he forgot why he was sitting by the pool and then he remembered the maid in the bathroom. The more he thought about it, the more he was beginning to think maybe it wasn't the young maid. He *wanted* it to be the young maid, but she actually seemed to be pretty careful about being alone around him. He assumed this was because she had a jealous boyfriend or something and someone with Barton's obvious assets was a great temptation to her and, therefore, a serious threat to her relationship. The wetbacks seemed to stick to themselves. This made him think maybe she wasn't cleaning his house at all. If that was the case, he'd have to bring it up to his parents or maybe William. One of them would deal with it. Tomorrow he'd be over at that house. He'd invited nearly 200 people and expected about 75. That was how these things usually worked. He'd started receiving the cancellations via email and text earlier in the week and had to take more pills than he usually did. And the pills really just helped curb the anxiety and anger. If he wanted to sleep he still typically needed to drink about a bottle of booze a night on top of the cocktails he enjoyed throughout the day.

His skin started to feel stretched and dry. He liked it. It made him think he was made of plastic. Not indestructible but with absolutely no feelings. No insides. It made him think of Mexico. He went down there a couple times a year to help out in the offices of his father's factories but mostly to vacation. Sometimes William went with him but he usually went alone. He liked to go places alone. Sometimes. Other times he wanted to be surrounded by people. Happy people. Fun people. Party people.

He looked up at the sun and saw three of those space birds circling it. One of them broke away from the other two and came toward him. He stayed in the chair until he could see that something dangling from its beak and then his heart started pounding and he had to get up and go inside, hit the wet bar, and pound some Grey Goose.

Now he felt moderately freaked out so he went back into the bedroom, picked up his phone, noticed three more cancellations along with a Facebook message from Jayne he'd have to come back to. He dialed his mom's number and it went straight to voice mail. He couldn't remember where they were vacationing, not that it really mattered. After the voice prompt, he said, "Do you remember when the butler's head turned into a balloon and he floated away?" Then he thought he heard a piece of paper ripping from their end of the phone so he terminated the call as quickly as possible.

He went back into the bathroom and the maid still lay on the floor.

"Hey, babe, you're gonna have to get up soon. I'm gonna need to shower. And I have to shit." He nudged her with his foot. Her eyes were open and her body had a kind of rag doll look to it. Now that he stood over top of her and looked at her face, not at her ass, he could tell it definitely was not the young one. He decided he would either tell his friends he'd fucked the young one or maybe tell them they wouldn't believe what an amazing ass this one had. Of course, if she was dead, he'd have to not say anything about it. He'd have to do something with the body. Or pay

William to do something with it. It was amazing what most people would do for money.

Looking at the maid made him think of Mexico again.

That made him think about tacos and piñatas.

Piñatas made him think about his party.

And candy.

He was going to the store to get some candy.

He pulled on some "casual" clothes he kept in a pile on the floor of his closet because that was where he assumed most poor people kept their clothes. A royal blue wife beater and cut off denim shorts cut short enough to allow just a portion of his scrotum to dangle free. He kept other accoutrements in a basket and selected a wig and a large pair of aviator sunglasses. People in this town were really close-minded and he preferred no one recognized him. He slid on his flip flops, grabbed his wallet and some cash and walked to the main garage, to his white Nissan Versa disguise car.

5.

Once he pulled out from the neighborhood and onto the state route, the booze and pills and sun hit him pretty hard and he had to slow way down. He closed one of his eyes so he could read the speedometer and stay on his side of the road. He thought maybe he forgot to shut the gate so he viciously jabbed at the remote control and hoped for the best.

One of those gross birds sat on the hood of his car so he turned on the windshield wipers.

He made it to the outskirts of town and decided he would just go to the Mexican store that was on this end. That would make it more authentic anyway. Maybe they could go with a Mexican theme. He could call the caterer and cancel the existing beer order. Maybe just get Corona. Maybe like ten kegs. And a bunch of those red cups. Then it would be just like the fraternity too. Double theme. Double fun. Double awesome. Potential name for a banner: MEXICO FRAT FUNLAND. And then maybe a subtitle: Take It Off!!!

Genius.

He had to pull the car to the side of the road so he could think about this for a couple of minutes. He wished Jayne hadn't turned out to be such a bitchy slut or he would have called her to tell her about it.

When he felt like he'd fully processed this change of plans and had a clear vision of all of his friends wandering around in Hawaiian shirts and cargo shorts, carrying red plastic cups, wasted on cheap tequila and Mexican drugs, all the girls with their tops off and their breasts flopping around, he pulled back onto the road and drove the remaining block to the corner store.

Getting out of the car he wished he'd worn his black wig so he fit in better. He felt so alienated being the only American there, not to mention the only one who spoke English. He walked in and the middle-age man behind the counter said, "Hello."

"Hola!" Barton smiled. He wasn't sure he could stop smiling.

They kept all of their candy right there at the counter. Barton grabbed box after box and sat them on the counter. He wasn't sure how much it would take but, once the counter was mostly covered, he thought he probably had enough.

He gestured to it and said, "Un mas soy cuanto poca!"

The clerk shrugged his shoulders, smiled bemusedly, and said, "Eh, I'm not sure."

Because some of the boxes were partially empty, the clerk had to count each piece of candy before entering them into the register. Watching the man's brown hand move all over the brightly colored little packages made Barton's stomach heave and he bent over and vomited onto the floor as covertly as he possibly could. He felt a lot better afterward.

He straightened up, felt the floor shift, managed to find the cash he kept in his pocket, grabbed the bags from the counter, tossed the cash to the clerk, and said, "Buy your family a fucking house."

He stepped outside, sat the bags on the ground, pulled his phone out of his pocket, and tweeted: "The sun is raping my eyes," which wasn't really true because he was wearing sunglasses and they worked pretty well, but he thought it was an amusing and interesting thing to say anyway. He put his phone in his pocket, struggled not to fall as he bent down to pick up the bags, and began walking toward his car. The driver's side door was open and music blared out from the speakers that were reasonably good for such a cheap car. He threw the bags in the back seat and slid into the driver's seat.

A dog sat in the passenger seat.

His pulse would have quickened if the drugs coursing through his body allowed that. Instead he just said, "Dog," and pulled his door shut. His dad would never let him have a dog and he felt bad making it get out in that apocalyptic heat. Actually, he didn't feel bad so much as he just didn't feel anything and continued doing what he would normally do if there wasn't a dog in the car. The worst thing about his dad not letting him have a dog was that he didn't even give him any kind of legitimate reason for it. He had just told him it wasn't a good idea like Barton was supposed to know what the fuck that meant. Like Barton had ever known what anything meant. As though he had ever been capable of finding the meaning in anything except his life as some kind of extension of his father's life, something that had to keep going, barreling forward until Barton could impregnate a woman, not with his child so much as his father's grandchild, so that *thing*, whatever it was, could continue to barrel forward long after he and his father were dead.

"This wig is making it hard to think," he said to no one or maybe the dog before putting the wig on the dog's head.

Barton thought about continuing into town to do some more shopping but he vaguely recalled giving William a list of things to pick up and felt it would probably be unnecessary for him to go out and pick up the same exact things. So he drove back home, half on the state route and half on the grass growing beside it. Halfway there, he finally decided to call Jayne. Despite the brutal nature of their breakup, she answered, and before she could say any more, he launched into his tirade.

"I can't believe you would do this to me, Jayne. You've left me all alone for the rats and space birds to feast upon. There's a dog in my car and I'm no longer wearing a wig. I feel so exposed. So *fucking* exposed. And used and cheap. You can forget about coming to Mexico Frat Funland. Consider yourself uninvited. And this was going to be fucking awesome, too. I got all of Team Klaus to DJ the fucking thing. Not just one of them. All fucking four of them, Jayne. Orange. Pink. Yellow. Blue. They're all going to be there making it the best and loudest fucking party this town has ever seen. And you're not going to see it. You're going to be at home with all of your Facebook friends shoved up in your vagina. Really crammed in there and you'll see how much they like you then when they're all covered in your pussy sweat. Do you think they know Mexico? Team Klaus I mean. Do you think they know Mexican music? Fuck this shit."

He tossed the phone in the passenger side floorboard.

The dog was still in the passenger seat.

A cop had just thrown on its sirens behind him.

He slowed down and pulled off on the side of the road. Since he was only going fifteen miles per hour and already half off the road, this was something he was able to manage. He rolled the window down, put both hands on the steering wheel, and pulled his lips back, baring his gleaming white, gritted teeth.

The officer approached the window and Barton handed him his wallet.

The cop pulled out the license and said, "Mister King. I didn't realize it was you." He handed the wallet back to Barton. "Cute dog. Have your dad call me when he gets back into town. I'll follow you home. Make sure you get there safely."

With the cop behind him making sure everything was okay, Barton felt protected and drove much faster. Occasionally he still swerved off the road and this sent the dog into something of a frenzy but he made it safely and didn't hit anybody head on. That would have been a drag. The cop drove on and tooted his horn when Barton reached the gates to his house which, yes, he'd left open and which the shitty low-powered remote control had not managed to close. He pulled up by the house and grabbed the candy and let the dog out of the car. The dog immediately bounded away, the wig falling off its head, and Barton headed to the bathroom with the candy to stuff that cunt of a maid.

6.

Alex lay next to Ibbie, staring at the ceiling. This was the first week they'd been able to sleep with the windows open and a soft breeze blew in and the heat made all the clean smells rise from the bed linens and he could smell the light sweat from Ibbie and the smell of her hair still trapped in his nostrils. He heard her pick up her phone from the nightstand before setting it back down and sighing. He put a hand on her delicious hip through the thin sheet and said, "What's wrong, babe?"

"Aunt Carla still hasn't called me back."

"Are you really that worried?"

"*Yes.* No. I don't know. She was the only one working there today."

Alex forced a laugh, tried to breathe some humor into the situation. "So maybe she just went out to try and forget about it."

"She *always* answers her phone."

"Maybe she's asleep. Maybe she didn't want to call you back and bother you. Do you think he'd really hurt one of

26

you?"

"Yes."

"I mean here. Or there. Whatever. In his own house?"

Ibbie had told Alex a lot about Barton King. He believed everything she said. Ibbie was probably the only woman he would believe unequivocally. He looked into her eyes and he could just tell. They'd been together for nearly a year and had lied to each other enough and seen through those lies enough that they didn't even bother doing it anymore. There wasn't a point. They were connected on that plane so few people are connected on. Alex liked it. He *loved* it. He loved *her*. He wouldn't have it any other way.

So he knew what the Kings did. More specifically, he knew what Barton King did. And he didn't really think there was anything he *wasn't* capable of, but he also knew rich people and knew that most of them exercised a weird conservative streak in their own homes.

"I mean," he said, "it's like the whole thing about not shitting where you sleep."

"I don't think he knows where he sleeps."

Alex lay there and chewed on his lip. He wanted to smoke again but if Ibbie wanted him to go out then he didn't want to be wasted. Joe was already asleep on their couch and therefore completely useless.

The Kings owned a number of factories in Mexico. Ciudad Juarez. Most of them specializing in clothing manufacturing. Barton was usually sent down when his parents were tired of dealing with him or just wanted the place to themselves. He had some kind of creepy handler named William. Ibbie thought Barton raped and murdered women on his trips. She had no reason to lie, but admitted she didn't have proof. She also believed he brought them back across the border. Either dumped them somewhere in the states or possibly even on the grounds of their expansive estate. When Alex thought about the amount of sod they'd laid down on the King estate, he was pretty sure what she said was true.

But he still couldn't see that stupid, drug addled rich kid killing someone who worked for them.

"If you're sure about this, we'll go over there."

Ibbie checked her phone and sighed and put the phone back down. "Just tell me I'm being stupid," she said.

He rubbed his hand along her thigh and said, "You're just concerned."

"Is that stupid?"

"Maybe." But he didn't know if he believed that or not.

7.

Barton shoved as much candy as he could down the maid's throat, in her ass, and up her cunt, but he still had like half a bag of candy left so he went to the kitchen to get a knife and wondered if he had a needle and thread, decided he didn't because that was what tailors were for so he got some duct tape instead.

He rolled the maid over onto her back and sliced her from the middle of her ribcage down to her hips. He had to squint his eyes. He expected blood to come pouring out but it was something like sunshine instead. It oozed out and stained her formerly light blue uniform a yellowish orange. And it glowed, radiating around the bathroom. Barton stood up and turned off the lights. He'd taken his sunglasses off and now put them back on. He looked at the bag of candy and then back at the maid. He felt inspired. He went back into his bedroom and hooked his laptop up to his super stereo system. He clicked on Team Klaus's mix called *No Bad Dreams in Sunshineland* and cranked the volume, felt the warm bass hum through his lungs.

He went back into the bathroom and finished stuffing the maid.

Taping her shut took the edge off some of the sunshine but the stuff that had stained her clothes was still glowing.

He still felt really good. He stripped off the maid's uniform and took it into his bedroom, turned off the lights, and slapped the uniform on the walls until they were pulsing with that light. Then he texted his friend Ben: "Dude U gotta get over here!"

Only a few seconds later, Ben texted back: "I've been in Canada for the past 3 months!"

Barton texted back: "U little bitch!" and wasn't sure if he was serious or not.

Ben never answered him so he stripped off his clothes and danced around the room by himself.

Things got really hazy. After hitting his wet bar and taking the fun dose of his pills, he tried to fuck the maid again but he couldn't get it up and couldn't get it in and quit. The music just kept going and it seemed like it was getting louder and developing colors or turning into clouds that floated around the room or something and at first it was soothing but then it became aggressive and almost violent and Barton tried to turn his laptop off but his hands were way too big and stiff so he had to rip the auxiliary jack out but that put a loud buzzing into his head and he couldn't get it to stop until he ripped the powerfully mounted Alain Silberstein clock from his wall and bashed the stereo with it and when he stood over the pile of shards in the middle of the room he realized the lights had faded from the walls and he was standing in complete and total darkness. The buzzing gave way to the tearing paper sounds. This time it was quick and furious and sounded just like it came from the middle of Barton's head. He needed to find out who was doing that. He needed to bash them with this clock. But he couldn't tonight. He vomited over the pile of stereo and managed to stagger over to his bed where he collapsed on top of the covers, thought the air conditioning was making it way too cold, and waited for the rats to come swarming out of the pipes and climb into bed with him and cover him up with their gross heat. He was disgusted and terrified but he couldn't move. These things had been in the toilet, in the pipes leading from the kitchen sink, below the bathtub. They were covered in shit and piss and blood and come and dead skin and dirt and human hair. Barton thought about taking a shower when he woke up.

8.

Alex stared at Joe until he woke up.

"Jesus, thought you were going to sleep all fucking day. Here. Put this shit on."

"What time is it?"

"It's like two."

"So thirsty."

"Fucking lightweight."

"Why are you wearing that?"

Alex wore a wig and sunglasses, a wife beater and obscenely cut off shorts.

"You're going to be wearing it too."

"Why?"

"Change of plans."

"Let me piss first."

Joe slowly got up from the couch and wandered toward the bathroom. The sound of his pissing filled the small apartment. It sounded like it lasted an hour. He came out carrying a dirty glass filled with dirty water. Sat down on the couch and lit a cigarette.

"So, change of plans?"

"Yep."

"So we're, uh, going to a costume party instead of breaking, entering, and robbing?"

"Nope. Still doing that. Although I don't think we'll really have to break in."

"Okay."

"It was Ibbie's day to work there today. Normally when the kid's home by himself she doesn't go. But her Aunt Carla wouldn't answer her phone last night and Ibbie wanted to make sure she was okay so she went in today."

"And ...?"

"Still not sure about her aunt but Ibbie said this Barton guy's completely out of his head. She's been hiding around the estate. She sent me some pictures of him. He pretty much looks like this. Meaning I think we can probably just walk into his house and take what we want. As long as we're not on camera at the same time outside of his house, we won't even have to really sneak too much."

"So if there's a safe in his house and he's having people over for a party, wouldn't it stand to reason that the safe is going to be locked?"

"Maybe and maybe not. Like I said, this guy's out of his head. Apparently the reason for the safe of cash is that his parents won't give him any credit cards. They probably don't want anything he does to be traced. People are going to be coming and going all afternoon and night. People who King is going to have to pay. Caterers. DJs. Drug dealers, probably. When Ibbie got there this morning, he'd left the front gates to his property wide open. So I'd say the chances of him leaving the safe open are pretty good. Man, this is going to be so easy and so untraceable."

"I think you're being naive."

"Naive? How so?"

"Well, the *only* thing rich people care about is money. That's how they got that way. If a bunch of money ends up missing, somebody is going to want to know where it went. And if we take all this guy's cash, how's he going to pay those other people?"

Alex laughed. "You're not seriously concerned about that, are you?"

"Yeah. If me and you did a job for somebody and we didn't get paid, I'd be pissed. Wouldn't you?"

"Okay, here's what happens if he doesn't have the cash to pay them ... Are you ready for this? It's fucking groundbreaking. They send him a fucking bill and whoever does the books pays them. It's that fucking simple."

"And this is all hinged on the hope that he's just leaving the safe wide open."

"Well, we have a backup plan."

Joe crushed out his cigarette. "Okay. Let's hear it."

Alex hissed out a breath. "Man, it's going to sound like I'm whoring her out or something. But you have to know how much I love Ibbie. If anything happened to her ..."

"Yeah, man, I know." Joe reached out and patted Alex on the shoulder. "I like Ibbie too. You guys are great together. I'm looking out for her too. But I gotta know what's going on."

"Okay. So Ibbie took a nice change of clothes with her. She's assuming if she's not wearing her uniform and puts on some make-up and fixes her hair or something King won't even recognize her. So if it's getting late into the night and the safe still hasn't been left open, she's going to come around and tell him she'd be willing to do some stuff for some cash."

"Jesus, that's a bad idea."

"She's not going to do anything. But he'll have to open the safe to get money and then she'll try and distract him and we'll move in. Or one of us will. If we're both supposed to be him then we probably shouldn't be seen together."

"So we just walk in and go to the safe and take all the cash and your girlfriend *might*, just might have to prostitute herself. And we'll be dressed like fucking retarded assclowns?"

"Pretty much."

"Best plan in the world. And I say that without a trace of sarcasm. I really do think this is the best plan in the world. It's not going to work. It sounds like something a twelve-year-old who's seen too many bank heist movies would come up with but, as far as like really lazy, easy things that have no foot or stake in reality go, it's really fucking good."

"I think it'll work. And look, if it's a disaster we'll probably know right away and then we'll get the fuck out. No harm done. If nothing's missing, no one's going to review the camera footage afterward. That's the way things work. They only record that stuff to review in the case of an incident. It's not a mall. There isn't some frustrated ex-cop in a booth watching this shit in between donuts, okay?

Oh, and get this, we'll be wearing sombreros too."

Joe lowered his head into his hands. "Do I need to ask why?"

"Because all these parties have themes, right? Like all rich people want to do is reenact the prom or something and the theme of this one is, get this, 'Mexico Frat Funland'."

"Oh God."

"Yeah, man, Ibbie saw it on his Facebook page. Aside from the Mexico part, it's everything we love. Fraternities, huh? Khaki shorts and date rape. You can't go wrong with that. And funland? Fuck. Who wouldn't like a funland? It's a land of fun filled with fun loving, attractive, plastic people. There isn't even any room for argument. It *is* funland."

"You sold that really well. Seriously. Whatever doubts I had are completely gone now. I'm looking really forward to going. I'm starting to think it's a shame we're going to have to rob this guy."

"That's the spirit!"

9.

The rats were gone by the time Barton woke up. He could hear the paper ripping (maybe in the attic) and a dog howling somewhere in the distance. Could have been that dog that rode with him from the store yesterday. He went into the bathroom to piss and shit and take a shower. The maid was still on the floor. He felt momentarily panicked and sad until he remembered she was filled with candy and sunshine. He would like to suspend the maid in the middle of the tent the caterers would be setting up. No, the caterers didn't set up the tent and the chairs and the tables. That was the party people. He was pretty sure they were called The Party People. They set up the tents and table and chairs. But not human piñatas. That was all him.

He was going to call William while he was shitting but he didn't have his phone on him. He needed his phone. There were so many people he needed to call. Also needed to see how many additional cancellations there'd been. Jesus, he still needed to make the banner. He thought it would probably be best if he did that himself. After all, that would be the first thing people saw and he couldn't really allow someone else to fuck it up. So then he needed to call the caterers and nix his previous order. The only things he wanted them to have on hand were fish tacos, churros, and Corona. Maybe he would jokingly tell them to leave the Mexican water at home. He needed William to bring him like a hundred sombreros. Everyone there, even the help, had better fucking wear a sombrero. Or else he'd like to carve out their eyes and stuff his testicles, his entire sack, into their eye sockets.

He moved from the toilet to the shower without wiping. What was the point?

He really wished he had a phone in the house so he didn't have to retrace his steps and try to find his cell phone. He hated looking for things. But his parents wouldn't let him have a phone in the house. He tried to tell them he didn't make crank calls anymore and they told him that wasn't the reason. Even thinking about it now made Barton irate. They never told him the reasons for anything. They just told him not to think about it so sometimes it felt like he went whole stretches of time without thinking about anything. Which reminded him he needed to take his pills. Today was going to be a high stress day with lots of people and lots of things to do so he decided he would take the fun dose and wash it down with some of the vodka. No, wait, he was already forgetting the theme. He'd wash it down with some tequila.

Then find his phone.

Check the cancellations.

Call William.

Fuck the maid again. Come all over her tits.

Call the caterers.

Call The Party People.

Call The Party People again and tell them what the caterers had done. Tell them they left things behind last time.

Call his parents.

Call his therapist. No. Fuck that. Today was Mexico Frat Funland. His therapist was a downer. He'd probably just try to tell him it wasn't a good idea.

Call all the people who'd canceled today and tell them how shitty it was to cancel at the last minute and try to guilt them into coming.

Call Team Klaus just to talk. Did they even speak English?

Find out where those ripping paper sounds were coming from and see if he could find that dog and get it out of here.

Make the banner.

No. He should probably do that first.

He rearranged the order of everything in his head.

Heard a dog howling.

Heard the ripping of paper.

Heard the rats scurrying in the pipes.

Closed his eyes and saw explosions of sunlight.

Smelled shit.

He'd forgotten to turn the water on.

10.

After showering, Barton tore all the clothes out of his closet looking for his favorite pink sweater. Maybe it was too warm to wear a sweater but he' planned on draping it artfully over his shoulders so it would be available if he got chilled later on. Once all the clothes were out of the closet and piled into an artless heap on his bedroom floor, he decided he didn't have a pink sweater, had only imagined having one, and went with a white one instead. He found one of several pairs of khaki cargo shorts left over from his real fraternity days, a light blue t-shirt that said, "Everyone loves a Mexican girl" (he'd crossed out "loves" and written "fucks" with a red Sharpie, but it was mostly illegible now), and, yes!, his shell necklace on a hemp band. He was going to be the realest looking person there. He quickly suited up and remembered to make the banner.

He Googled "make banner" and clicked on the first website it gave him. He didn't have the time to go through all the fonts and backgrounds. Maybe he'd decorate it later. He picked the biggest font he could. That would make it eye catching at least. He went with a different color for every letter and hit print. Unfortunately his printer was out of color cartridges so it just printed black on white, one letter per page. Maybe he'd put William to work on it if his lazy ass ever decided to show up.

That reminded him he still needed to get his phone out of the car.

He ran down there as fast as he could. By the time he reached the car he was panting and out of breath, the sun attacking him. He braced himself on the car so he didn't fall down. He saw the dog who'd ridden home with him yesterday on the far side of the pool, carrying something in his mouth. This didn't look as meaty as whatever it was the space birds carried. It looked more like a bone.

He saw the maid (this time he was pretty sure it was the young one) walking toward the main house. He thought about running after her and tackling her, maybe raping her or possibly just tickling her until she pissed herself.

He opened the car door and grabbed his phone. He needed to get back inside to the air conditioning before he passed out.

First he needed to call William. Shit. The phone was dead. Now he'd have to find the charger too. He hated looking for things. Maybe he would go to the main house and use the landline phone. But then he'd have to go out in that sick heat again. He'd definitely pass out by the time he made it to the main house. And he hadn't seen any of those birds today which meant they were probably all gathered together and conspiring. They'd probably swarm when everyone else showed up. He didn't know if that would be embarrassing or cool.

The charger was plugged into the wall next to the bed. The rationality of this location struck him as nearly absurd.

Once his phone turned back on, the cancelation messages started popping up. They overwhelmed him and he lay down on the bed, careful to make sure there weren't any rat droppings on it.

At this point it was probably easier to think about who *would* be there. Chris would come. Chris came to everything because, even though he was nearly thirty, he still lived with his parents. Like in the same house with them, not in a separate house on the same estate. There wasn't anything wrong with that.

Jordan.

Jordan would probably come. Barton was going to finally break it to him that he had a girl's name. Meaning Barton could either fuck him in the mouth or call him Joe, which Barton thought was manlier and more generally traditional sounding. Jordan would come because he was on drugs and an alcoholic and usually didn't have a lot of money. Barton always had all of those things.

Polly.

Polly would come because, well, she was a twenty-something girl named Polly. And she was kind of fat and not very attractive and probably didn't get invited out a lot. Maybe he and Jordan and Chris would pull a train on her. That might be kind of fun. He hadn't done that in a while. They'd have to drag her back to his house where there weren't any cameras because even though she'd probably be totally into it she'd still cry rape afterward unless she felt too ashamed but, given the way she looked, he thought she would probably feel more pride than shame. But Barton had a lot of money, which made him the target of so many people who wanted that money.

That was it. He couldn't think of another person who was guaranteed to come.

Maybe Andy.

But Andy was virtually nonexistent. Maybe he'd show up. Maybe he wouldn't. Barton probably wouldn't notice if he was there or not.

He called William.

William never answered his phone. Barton just left messages and he showed up.

"William, buddy, hope you're going to be here soon."

Barton ended the call and made some of the other calls he'd planned. Many of the people he spoke with seemed jumbled and confused, as though they'd invented a new language. This, in turn, made Barton jumbled and confused, so when he ended what he thought was his last call, he went to the bar and took the fun dose of his pills and washed it down with some tequila. Then he went to the bathroom and rolled around with the maid again before taking another shower, this time with his clothes on.

He got out of the shower and vomited red into the toilet. At first he was concerned until he remembered drinking some of the maid's blood. He'd have to throw up again later and see what it looked like. A flash of brilliance struck him and he removed his sopping, heavy sweater from around his neck and dropped it into the toilet. He reached his hands in and massaged the sweater so it would soak up some of the bloody vomit, moderately terrified that a rat was going to bite one of his fingers off. He wrung the sweater over the toilet, pleased that it was close to the shade of pink he'd imagined.

A honking horn disrupted his admiration.

His first thought was that it was the police and he should hide. Then he wondered why he would think that. He didn't have anything to worry about. He refastened the sweater over his shoulders and went downstairs and outside to see who was honking.

A black, unmarked van was up near the main house. The keys were still in the Versa, so he got in and drove it to the main house. He was pretty sure the only things he would need from his house were the maid and the banner. No. He should probably get the banner now so when people started showing up, they would know they were at the right place. Of course, when he'd sent out the elaborate invitations, it hadn't been called MEXICO FRAT FUNLAND. He couldn't remember what it used to be known as. He whipped the Versa around, skidded to a stop in front of his house, and ran upstairs to grab the banner. His Alain Silberstein clock was lying on the floor for some reason and he decided to grab that too. Hoisting it up sent an explosion of sunshine through his head. He thought of the maid but wasn't sure why. He remembered his phone was still plugged in and charging. He grabbed the phone and the cord. The banner hadn't been taped together yet so it was just a small stack of paper. Now his hands felt too full. Where the fuck was William?

"William!" he shouted at the ceiling.

He was greeted only by the ripping of paper and the scurry of rats.

He walked everything out to the car and tried his hardest not to break down into tears.

11.

He drove to the main house as fast as he could. Standing beside the black van were four dour looking men dressed identically in black shirts and black pants. The only variation between the four were the matching colors of their ties and shoes. Team Klaus. Had to be. Barton had never noticed the shoes before. Beside them stood a man in a gray business suit, probably their manager. Barton was glad he wore his disguise. While he would have happily gushed over them, he would have also been embarrassed if they knew he had to deal with those affairs himself. He glanced toward the house and noticed the maid, definitely the young hot one, in the large breakfast nook window.

"Mr. King." The man in the gray suit held out his hand. "I'm Buddy Reynolds, manager of Team Klaus."

"I'm not ..." Now Barton found it hard to think about anything except the maid in the window. "I mean ... I'm William." He held out his hand and the man in gray took it.

"Nice to meet you, William. I'm sure Mr. King made you aware of the agreed upon price. We can go ahead and get that out of the way."

"I ... yes. Cash good."

"Cash is great. We'll give you a receipt if you need it."

"No." Barton thought about the drive back to his house and then the drive back here and he nearly fell over. He wanted to cry. Maybe he could get the young maid to do it. Maybe he could do other stuff with her when he got her into his house. "Maid! Maid! Maid! Maid!" he shouted at the house. The man in the gray suit flinched back. Team Klaus remained stony, staring somewhere in the middle distance.

"Is everything okay ... William?" the man in the gray suit asked.

Barton pressed the heels of his hands against his eyes. He could hear the sound of ripping paper float over the expansive lawn as though it were waiting for him.

"I'll go get it. The cash. The maid is a lazy Mexican."

The man looked confused, like he hadn't quite heard him, so Barton grabbed him by the upper arms and yelled, "The maid is a lazy Mexican!"

The man knocked Barton's hands off and straightened his suit. His eyes had hardened, all good manners and politeness gone. "We'll start setting up then. Where would you like us?"

Barton pointed his finger at the large stone patio and said, "Anywhere over there."

Two other men in black coveralls and gas masks climbed out of the van carrying a mess of cords and walked toward the patio. Barton got into the Versa and sped back to his house. He went upstairs and to the sitting room just off his bedroom, took the oil painting of dogs playing poker off the wall and opened the safe. He never locked it. He'd forgotten the combination a long time ago because his dad wouldn't let him write it down. He had no idea how much money he would need and wasn't sure he could count at this point anyway. He went downstairs and got his suitcase from the storage closet off the kitchen. Back upstairs he emptied as much of the money as he could into the suitcase. Most of it was still in bundles so he was sure he had an ample amount. He left a couple of bundles in the safe just in case. Also because there was a rat in the very back of the safe, hunkered over, nose twitching, probably hungry, and he didn't want to accidentally touch it. He mumbled, "Rats are only for sleeping," before zipping up the suitcase and heading back to the car amidst the cacophony of ripping paper.

On the way back out to the car, he spotted the dog again. This time it wore a human skull like a hat and Barton was pretty sure the dog was making fun of him.

He got in the car, cried for a few minutes, and sped back to the main house.

William stood in front of the black van talking to Team Klaus's manager. It looked like the man, Barton couldn't remember his name, was at ease again. William had an amazing ability to connect with just about anyone. Whatever it was William did, he was very good at it.

"Hey, William," William said. The manager must have told him Barton had introduced himself as William and the real William, being as quick as he was, must have picked up on it. Barton also realized he wasn't wearing his disguise like he'd originally thought and was doubly happy to have pulled off the ruse.

Barton almost felt like breaking down again, he was so happy to see William and his deeply lined face and wise eyes.

"I'm so glad you're finally here." Barton hoisted the suitcase full of cash at him. "Here, you deal with this now. I've got something I need to do."

"What's that smell?" William asked.

"That's the smell of fun. Mexico Frat Funland."

Barton went back to the car and got his clock and the loose pages he would need to tape to make his banner. He went into the kitchen. The table in there was probably the largest surface in the house. He heard the maid cough from somewhere upstairs. He sat down the papers for the banner, held onto the clock, and followed the sound.

12.

Joe and Alex sat on the couch, each of their right arms raised in front of them, obliterating the zombies on the screen. They had wanted to spend the day wasted, as they usually did on their days off, but knew they needed to remain sharp. Therefore it had been nothing but coffee and energy drinks and they were both feeling pretty giddy and wired. Alex hit pause and grabbed his phone from his pocket.

"Dude, it's Ibbie. She just sent a message that says, 'Come now.'"

Joe looked at him, frozen.

"We should probably go. Get the wigs and stuff."

Other than the wigs, they were both already in costume. Alex disappeared into the kitchen and came back out with a gun.

"What the fuck's that?"

"It's a gun."

"Is it real?"

"Yeah, man, it's real."

"Do you even know how to use that?"

"Mostly."

"Mostly?"

"Look. It's a precaution. I'm not planning on using it."

"But you realize just by taking that it makes what we're doing even ... more illegal. Like if you have a weapon we'll spend ten more years in jail."

"It might save our lives."

Joe stopped. "Look at who you're talking about. It sounds like it would be like shooting a retarded kid in a wheelchair. I'm not going if you're taking the gun."

Maybe it was just the immediacy of Ibbie's message but Alex really wanted to take the gun. He didn't have time to rationalize it. But he also didn't want to go alone. Ibbie probably wasn't in any kind of danger. If she were in great danger, he didn't think she'd have the time to stop and whip off a text. Maybe King had stepped out. Maybe Ibbie just knew they'd be in the apartment not really doing much anyway and decided now would be a good time to try something. Apparently King always left the house in disguise. That would be too perfect. The cameras see him leaving in disguise and then coming back looking the same way.

Alex took a deep breath. Convinced himself he didn't need the gun. Gently placed it on the couch between the two fake guns.

"There. Satisfied?"

"We don't need it."

"If one of us or Ibbie gets hurt, I'm blaming you. Understand?"

"I'll take the heat, man. Everything'll be fine. Or as fine as it could be with your idiot plan."

"No faith."

"Got that right."

13.

Barton was pretty sure the cough had come from upstairs. He paused before ascending the staircase. What if the cough was like the paper sounds? What if he searched and searched for it but never found it? What then? Then Mexico Frat Funland would be a complete bust. He'd already decided there would be as many DJs as guests and that was completely humiliating. But if he *were* able to capture the beautiful young maid, then it seemed like that would be the *very definition* of Mexico Frat Funland. He could probably pay or force her to do just about anything. Strip. Wet t-shirt. Maybe they could *all* fuck her. He'd been to a couple of parties like that in college. Had never gotten to indulge though. Sometimes if he drank too much he couldn't get hard and to try and participate in front of that many people only to fail would have been so embarrassing he'd had to have left school. Luckily, since then he'd discovered Viagra. It didn't matter how much he drank or how fun his dose of other pills was, if he took enough Viagra, he'd remain rock hard.

Mexico Frat Funland.

Legendary.

He wondered what time it was.

He'd set his phone alarm under the new title, "Party Time," and it hadn't gone off yet. Of course, it was probably dead. He had the phone and the cord in his pocket. He sat the clock down on the first step. He turned his phone on and was surprised to see the screen come to life. There must have been a tiny amount of power left. He called William. Barton was surprised he answered. He must have sensed the urgency of ... everything. Barton told him about the piñata in his bathroom. Told him he wanted it suspended from one of the beams in the middle of the hut on the patio because, obviously, The Party People were not going to show up with their tent and chairs. Where he'd told the DJs to set up? Of course where he'd told the DJs to set up. Where else would they expect them to hang a piñata? From the sky? If you try and hang things from the sky, they'll get all pecked at by space birds.

"I feel alive, William. I feel so fucking alive!"

And he did, momentarily anyway.

He plugged his phone in in the kitchen and left it on the counter. He went back to the staircase and grabbed his clock. It was very dense and metal. He could grip it in his hand but it was almost too heavy. He began climbing the stairs. The farther he went up, the darker it got. He thought it was probably just clouds moving over the sun and he imagined the winding stairway as a tunnel and it made him think of when he would go down to the basement of their massive house in New York when he was a kid. It was the first house he could remember. He would go into the basement with an aluminum baseball bat in search of rats. They were all over in that house. They didn't come out of the pipes and sleep with him like they did here. They knew their place. And he would pretend that his baseball bat was a sword and his name was the White Lord and if he could rid the village of rats, all those rats that didn't belong there, he would be adored by the villagers and given his pick of the fairest virgin to take to bed. Eventually waiting for the rats in the basement wasn't good enough. He wanted to catch them at their source. He found a spot in the woods where he could enter the sewers. He would go in and not come back out until all the rats had been killed. He'd gotten lost in the sewers and some city workers had to come and find him. *They* were the ones who'd told him he'd gotten lost. Probably sent to him by his parents. But Barton hadn't gotten lost. He'd found some essential part of himself that his parents and most other people wouldn't understand. He felt fine. He felt perfect. He felt almost invincible. It was his parents who were always taking him to the doctor and trying to convince him he was sick.

Barton shifted the clock to his left hand and came out at the top of the tunnel.

There was sunlight all around him.

He looked for the maid but he could barely see anything.

Maybe she was sunlight. Maybe she was all around him.

His heart raced in his chest and he felt like crying again.

He lay down on the bed and pulled the clock up to his chest. He tried to make it call his parents but it must have been dead. Either the clock or his parents. They didn't make phones like they used to.

14.

"These shades are really nice," Joe said.

They were in the car on their way to the King estate. The day was violently sunny. Alex was grateful for the sunglasses too. The car didn't have air conditioning so the wig was another story. Even with all the windows down he could still feel the sweat saturating his real hair.

"Do you think we should maybe find out if Ibbie's in trouble?" Joe asked.

Alex tossed him the phone. "You do it. I don't want to text and drive."

Joe picked the phone up from in between his legs and stared at it. "What should I say?"

"How about 'Are you okay?'"

It felt like it took Joe half an hour to type this in. After hitting send he continued to stare at the phone.

"You don't have to stare at it," Alex said. "It'll vibrate if she sends one back." Joe was maybe the last person on the planet who didn't own a cell phone. He'd always told Alex that if he had a cell phone he'd have to pay for anxiety medication *and* a cell phone plan.

They passed through downtown, careful not to roll through any stop signs or go even a mile per hour above the speed limit. King didn't live in a gated community because, essentially, anything from the center of downtown east was an entire gated community. The cops who were on duty were there to protect the rich folks who lived up in the hills. And there were more cops than in your average small town. Everyone's tax dollars going toward the visibility of cops so the rich had at least the illusion of safety. Besides, a gated community would have been redundant, since all the houses were gated and secure anyway. Doing the lawn and garden work in this area had given both Alex and Joe a good sense of how these people operated. Most of the estates, they wouldn't even contemplate doing something like this. But the King place seemed to be designed to be taken advantage of. Well, maybe not the place, but that kid certainly was. Alex didn't really know why he continually thought of him as a kid, since Barton was probably older than him. Actually, Alex tended to think of every male in this area as a kid. They were all like big overgrown children who were paying to be pampered. That's why all the women were either frumpy, stereotypical soccer moms or catalogue attractive in that silicone and heavily artificial way. In short, the type of women twelve-year-old boys usually found attractive.

But Alex guessed it wasn't just the rich who were like that. Even his poor and working class brethren were a bit stunted in their emotional development with their guns and sports and motorcycles.

The phone vibrated. "Oh," Joe said.

"What does it say?" Alex fought the urge to rip the phone out of Joe's hands.

"'Not immediately.'"

"Tell her we're almost there."

Joe typed in "astolm thare" and hit send.

It was hard for Alex not to speed. He didn't really think Ibbie was in serious danger, but she wasn't one to exaggerate. If anything, she downplayed things. This made him even a little more nervous.

"Whoa." Joe was looking at the phone again.

"What?"

"It says, 'Think about calling the police.'"

"Give me the phone."

Joe handed it over. Alex tapped Ibbie's name and listened to the phone ring and ring and then go to voice mail. "Please call me back and tell me what's going on." He tapped end call and put it on the seat between his legs. It vibrated almost immediately and he picked it up. He held it with both hands so he could read and drive.

He read out loud. "Can't talk. If I talk he'll hear me. His parents are dead in the house. Pretty scared."

"I don't like this," Joe said.

"What do we do?"

"Call the fucking police."

They were now only a couple of miles from King's, already out of town where the houses were spread acres apart, huge mature trees populating the lots. Most of the houses weren't even visible from the road. Alex knew the serenity was only a facade. There were cameras and infrared laser beams all over the place. People watching from secret rooms and, the houses – the ones that could be seen – while projecting the warm glow of happiness and peace and tranquility, were undoubtedly ablaze with anxiety. He had yet to meet a rich person who got rich from doing something he or she felt good about. It seemed that in order to get rich, you had to take advantage of a lot of people in order to construct that solid gold house of cards.

He wanted to pull over and think about calling the police, maybe talk this over with Joe, but if he pulled off to the side of the road or, even worse, into the end of one of their driveways in his little piece of shit car, they wouldn't *have* to call the police because they'd be pulling up behind his car within a matter of seconds.

And maybe that was what he was afraid of.

Maybe if a cop showed up, he'd tell the cop he had a girlfriend who worked for the Kings and said there was some really weird shit going on right now. Or, no, maybe that wouldn't sound serious enough. Maybe they wouldn't even be able to investigate that. So maybe Alex would tell a cop that Ibbie was in trouble.

And then he could kiss the money goodbye. Saved or spent he'd already planned on that money going toward a better life for him and Ibbie.

And just as he thought he might be a complete and total idiot, Joe confirmed it by asking, "What are we going to do with the car?"

Although, in his way, that was Joe confirming he was still on board with the original plan.

"I'll stop the car just before his house and we'll have to

switch. I'll give you the phone and walk up to the house. If you don't hear from me in ten or fifteen minutes, text Ibbie. If she doesn't text back, feel free to call the police but text or leave a message letting us know. If we *are* in there and don't need the police, I don't want to be caught doing anything stupid when they do show up. Got all that?"

"Sure."

And Alex knew he probably did.

He pulled the car over.

15.

Maybe he was out for a couple of minutes because he hoped what he had seen was a dream.

The sky was bright but he couldn't see the sun because it was covered by the space birds. There must have been thousands of them up there. And he was being lifted toward them and looked down to see what was doing the lifting even though it made him so dizzy he felt like he might fall.

Rats.

As many rats below him as there were space birds above him and he wished he had his baseball bat.

They lifted him higher and higher until he thought they were feeding him to the space birds. Then all the space birds dispersed and the sun exploded. They began flying toward him and he saw that the sun hadn't exploded. They'd ripped it apart.

And then the rats were gone and he was falling.

Catching himself.

Prying his eyes open. The evening sun blasted through the window and he realized his glasses must have fallen off while he was out, if he'd even been wearing them. He climbed out of the bed. The room stunk. He hadn't been up here in a couple of weeks but it smelled worse than he remembered. Except there was another scent too.

Was it the scent he had followed up here?

No. He had followed the sound of a cough up here, but that scent had been here too. He must have had a hard time trying to distinguish it from the smell of rot.

The sound of paper ripped down the hall. It was so loud Barton had to bring his hands up to his ears, almost knocking himself out with the clock he still clutched in his hand.

He was sure whoever was ripping paper had been doing it from his house. Over there, he hadn't seen how it could get any louder.

But there it was again and it felt like someone jabbing a spike into his skull. A spike with an amplifier on the end of it.

He got out of the bed, located his glasses, and adjusted his wig. He switched the clock to his left hand and followed the sounds of ripping paper – almost furious now – down the hall.

Once in the hall, he had to orient himself. He'd stepped out of his parents' bedroom. Why was he there? He had absolutely no idea. Maybe he was just tired. But he was waiting for the party to start. Now was not the right time to be tired. He *shouldn't* be tired. He should be happy. He should be energized and ecstatic.

Mexico Frat Funland!

It was going to be great!

Already he'd lost track of what he was doing. The deafening sound of ripping paper tore through his skull again and he was reminded. It was coming from in here. He was going to find whoever was doing that and fuck them up. He lifted the clock in his hand to make sure he could effectively use it as a weapon.

The only rooms toward that end of the hall were a guest room and his father's study. He didn't know why anyone would be in his father's study with his father away on vacation. It was possible someone was in the guest room. Maybe it was a relative that had come over and decided to crash there. Maybe they hadn't told Barton or maybe they had and he'd since forgotten. Or maybe some of the help had decided to stay there since they knew Barton's parents would be out of town. That seemed liked something they would do. Probably had a whole family living in there. He remembered seeing the maid down in the kitchen and following her cough. That was probably why she was here. There were probably a whole bunch of them living here. Living it up while his parents were gone.

Part of Barton wished the maid *was* in there. He had a clock and, if he popped one or two of his Viagras, he could have a hard-on very shortly. Maybe it wasn't a bad idea to be proactive. He stopped his march down the hall, reaching into his pocket, glad he'd remembered to put the bottle in there. It was the only drug he'd bothered bringing. It wasn't a sure thing but Barton liked to think sex was somehow central to just about any party. He dry mouthed the pills and continued walking.

He reached the heavy wooden door of his father's study

and almost knocked on the door. But that was stupid. He didn't need to knock on the door. This was practically his house. And he was the only one with any right to be here. Well, maybe William could be in here but Barton would pretty much let William do anything he wanted.

He opened the door slowly, brandishing the clock in front of him.

The first things he noticed were the glossy black and white photos of dead rats pinned or taped to the bookcases lining the room. Maybe his father had turned his study into something like a dark room. But why would he choose to take pictures of dead rats? It seemed gruesome.

Then he noticed his father sitting behind the desk. He didn't look very good. He almost looked dead. Like a zombie. His head was bent down as if studying something on the desk. When Barton stepped farther into the room, his father lifted his head.

"Barton," he said, "we need to have a talk."

"I'd love to, Dad, but I'm kind of in the middle of something very important –"

The sound of ripping paper almost took him to his knees.

"I thought that might get your attention." His father held a piece of paper in his hands. "Do you know what that sound is?"

Barton's eyes felt unfocused. "It's ripping paper. I've been hearing it for weeks."

"That's right. It's also the sound of you going from being one of the wealthiest people in the state to being absolutely destitute."

Barton laughed and stared frantically around the room.

"I don't even know what that means."

"*Poor*, Barton. It means you're going to be poor, without anything. Including a home. I want you out by the end of the week."

His father tore another piece of paper. Barton remembered now. Kind of. It was the will he was tearing up. Along with a lot of Barton's trust fund paperwork. His father had told him he couldn't have a trust fund if he couldn't be trusted and Barton had thought that was kind of corny but maybe kind of cool. And then his father had pulled out a folder and began showing him photo after photo of dead rats. Rats half buried in the ground. Rats hanging from trees. A dead rat in the trunk of a car. A charred rat.

Barton was surprised by the clarity of that memory, especially when he couldn't seem to remember just a few seconds ago. But that day stood out. It was essentially the day his parents told him they didn't love him. Only his mother wasn't there. His father had probably sent her away. But she'd come back later. Barton confronted her about the space birds. Asked them how else they'd gotten those pictures when his mom denied she even knew what a space bird was. And then she told Barton he had broken their hearts and the last thing he remembered was reaching for her and the sun exploding through the windows in the room and ...

... and then everything had been just great.

He didn't know why he had to work himself up over things like this. He looked around his father's study. There weren't any photos of dead rats hanging there. His father wasn't behind the desk. He was on vacation. On vacation with Barton's mother. Probably for a long time.

Barton straightened himself up as best he could.

His heart hammered and he might have been crying but he had a party to get to.

Mexico Frat Funland.

Rock on.

16.

Having done most of his work in the gardens and shrubbery surrounding the estate, Alex was able to get out of the driveway as soon as he walked onto the property. Everything was almost mathematically even spaced to give them room to work on everything, not that they really did much of anything on a regular basis except mow the grass. Most of the other time was just spent slacking. The only time the residents ever paid any attention to the trees and the gardens was in the spring when it wasn't too hot to be outside and everything was fresh and new to look at. Then they would call the company and complain if something didn't look perfect and a "technician" would come out and remove the offending weeds or dead leaves.

Once he was closer to the house he glanced over at what he and his coworkers usually referred to as the party patio. Alex was pretty sure it was larger than his entire apartment complex. There weren't a lot of people over there. It looked like the beginnings of just about any other rich get together. Although this one seemed like it was going to be pretty low-key with not that many attendees. There were some DJs hooking up their equipment. Amidst them was that creepy guy, William, who was up on a ladder and fooling around with something in the rafters of the patio's thatch-like cover. There were a couple of other people milling around and drinking out of those red plastic cups. Alex noted how college that was immediately before seeing the wholly undecorative banner strung at the entrance to the party patio: MEXICOD TARF FUNLAN. The banner wasn't particularly meaningful but it made him remember how he and Joe had shared a laugh over the theme of the party. He wanted to laugh again but now, up close to it, it just seemed more sad than anything else. Also, he realized he'd forgotten to wear a sombrero.

He didn't see any sign of King and that didn't make him feel any better. He needed to find Ibbie. Maybe leaving the phone with Joe hadn't been the best idea. He'd forgotten how expansive the estate was. If she thought he'd called the police when she told him he should have, then she could be hiding anywhere, probably just making sure she was safe until after the police had left.

Or she had left.

That seemed like the logical thing to do. Especially if she felt like she was in danger.

Unless ...

Unless she wanted the money as much as he did. Even if it was only a few thousand dollars it could change things drastically for them.

It hadn't even occurred to him to check the safe before looking for Ibbie but, now that he thought about it, he felt guilty.

Keeping to the narrow mulched trail between the landscaping and the twelve-foot high wrought iron fence, Alex walked toward the guesthouse, hoping he spotted Ibbie before he made it there. After taking a few steps, a loud rumble shook the ground. He was alarmed for a second until more syncopated rumbles followed it and he realized the DJs had started playing. He looked back toward the party patio. Beyond that he noticed the sun was gone from the sky and it would only be light for a few more minutes.

17.

The whole house exploded with sunlight and then the sunlight was gone and the automatic, artificial lights began clicking on. Barton staggered downstairs. It seemed like the last few minutes, maybe even the whole last day, had been an almost nightmarish jumble of thoughts. Now he was only thinking about one thing.

Having fun.

In a way reminiscent of his college fraternity days and Mexico, that great country, the land of rats.

He made it into the kitchen and saw Polly and Chris standing there. They were gathered around the island and drinking something out of red plastic cups. He really hoped it was tequila or beer.

"Hi guys," Barton said. "Thanks for waiting on me. What's in those cups?"

"I don't know," Chris said. "Whatever beer you had on tap out there. Heineken, maybe?"

"I had that guy in the suit make me a screwdriver."

Barton put the clock down on the counter and clutched

the sides of his head with his hands. Thankfully, he hadn't heard the ripping of paper since coming downstairs.

"You guys," he said, "are just the sloggiest bunch of friends ever. Polly – please tell me how what you're wearing is in any way Mexican or fraternity themed."

She held her arms away from her body and inspected her, dear god, velour running suit stretched over her abundant curves. Although, really, Barton felt it was too generous to describe them as curves. They were just fat piles. She was a bronzy velour covered collection of fat piles.

"I didn't know there was a theme."

Barton gritted his teeth. "There's always a theme. You look like a teaser image for a BBW website. And Chris, you? How are you dressed for the theme?"

"Dude, I didn't know it was a costume party."

Barton closed his eyes and picked up his clock. "Let's go outside ... to the beach." He hadn't had time to actually have the sand trucked in but it had occurred to him. Chris and Polly were so unresponsive to the theme they probably wouldn't even care.

Polly took a sip of her screwdriver and led the way. Chris turned behind her and Barton was ready to club him in the back of his head before the maid entered the kitchen. Maybe she thought she was safe now that there were other people here. The bass from Team Klaus kicked in, scaring Barton for a second, and he reached out his free hand surprisingly quickly for someone with that amount of drugs in him, and grabbed the maid's arm. His penis was rock hard in his pants and he remembered the Viagra he'd taken.

"Welcome to Mexico Frat Funland, bitch! It's a good thing we have some authentic Mexicans for the entertainment." He leaned in to her fabulous scent. "Don't worry, honey, I'll make it worth your while."

"I'm Colombian," Ibbie said.

"Whatever. Same thing."

She screamed but Barton doubted anyone other than those in the immediate vicinity heard her.

Ibbie struggled but his grip was like a vice. The group filed out to the patio.

18.

Alex scanned his surroundings carefully before coming out of hiding. He didn't know what he expected. This was someone's home. Not a place of business. There wouldn't be employees wandering around at all times. But he knew that wasn't necessarily true. Most of the homes of the wealthy he'd been in were exactly like businesses. All he had to do was look at what he did. His basically nine to five day was spent at other people's houses doing things he would do at his own house if he could afford one. It almost seemed like they expressly tried to turn their home lives into something resembling work. Otherwise it seemed like they'd just get some small affordable place and spend their huge amounts of money on traveling or doing things. Nothing they did made sense. If he had a lot of money, the last thing he would have wanted to be was a fucking clone. The only way they knew if something was truly unique was by how high it was priced.

He didn't see anybody. The music continued to hum along. He didn't know who they were but he kind of liked it. It still didn't make any sense why a person would pay for a group of electronic musicians to come and play live electronic music or spin songs that he could just put on a playlist.

Alex wandered to the entrance of the guest house, trying to look like he belonged. It was hard to feel like he belonged anywhere while wearing the sunglasses, ridiculous wig, and cut off shorts. He hoped Ibbie would recognize him and approach him if she did.

He pulled on the front door and it opened. Not even locked. Of course, why would you if your house was surrounded by a giant fence with razor wire looped around the top?

As soon as he stepped inside, everything went dark.

He quickly backed out of the house. He didn't know if he did that so he could glance back at the main house and make sure the lights were out there too or if he thought somehow his entering the house had made the lights turn off.

The lights were out at the main house.

They were out everywhere.

A security light buzzed somewhere around the pool but it didn't throw off much light.

Before, Alex had been scared for Ibbie, wanting to know if she was okay. He hadn't really been worrying about himself.

Now he did.

It seemed like there were just too many odd things happening. Or maybe there wasn't *enough* happening. There really should be more people here. There should have been more going on.

He cursed himself for not bringing a flashlight or, again, his phone. His phone had a flashlight app on it. He could have used that. He wondered if Joe had made contact with Ibbie yet. He should have predetermined a place to be and told Joe to text Ibbie with that location. Any of them probably knew the estate better than the Kings. If he had Ibbie's job, he would have probably forged ahead in the dark and tried to find the safe anyway. But he was responsible for the dirt and the grass and the flowers outside of the house.

He was almost grateful for the darkness. It gave him an excuse not to go in. He was kind of afraid.

He began walking toward the main house.

19.

Out on the patio Barton stared at the strip of lingering sunlight limning the western horizon with a glazed expression.

"Anybody seen William?" he asked no one in particular.

No one answered him. He thought maybe they didn't know who William was.

"You know ... William? The guy ... with the ... *fuck* ... Wanna go see the piñata?"

"Fuck yeah," Chris said. "I love piñatas. Does it have candy in it?"

"Shit yeah."

He thought about marching them over to the piñata and then remembered the maid he clutched in his left hand. He'd been clutching her so long and so hard that one or both of them had started to sweat. He liked the feeling. He shook her by the arm.

"I told you you were going to be part of our entertainment tonight, didn't I?"

The stupid bitch didn't say anything at all. Maybe it was

one of those things where she thought anything she could say would probably incriminate her in some way. Whatever way she answered would be the wrong way. But Barton really just wanted to hear her voice.

"You ever done a striptease before?" he said. "Of course you have. Probably stripped your way into this country."

"I was born here."

Barton laughed and said, "That's funny."

Barton envisioned her stripping in front of Team Klaus. They had brought some moderate visual effects, mostly just lights complementing their individual colors and Barton thought it would look cool. But he knew the second he let her go, she would take off running. Where was William? William usually carried a gun. He could have made William stand guard while she danced and took off her clothes. His cock was so hard. Maybe he wouldn't make her strip. Or maybe he wouldn't make her *just* strip. If he promised Chris he could have sex with her too then maybe he would guard her, keep her from getting away. He really wanted to show them the piñata.

The last of the day's glow left the sky and Barton looked up to see more space birds than ever circling. He waited to hear the sound of ripping paper but didn't think he'd be hearing that anymore. He'd put an end to that a while ago and wondered why he'd heard it for so long after. Maybe because he'd forgotten about putting an end to it. He half-hooted and half-howled and said, "Let's go bust that piñata."

Chris shrieked something and hoisted his red cup into the air. Polly did the same.

"I don't have a stick or anything so we'll have to bust it with this clock. I'll go first."

They continued walking toward the band. Each member of the band continued to labor his respective keyboard, turntable, or drum machine. Part of Barton was really excited to see Chris and Polly's reactions when they saw the piñata. He climbed up on the small raised stage (Team Klaus must have brought that with them) and gestured toward the piñata.

William had done a good job.

The maid started screaming and trying to get away.

Chris said, "Is that ...?"

Polly said, "That's sick, Barton. I hope it isn't really."

The DJs continued to play.

The grounds went dark.

Barton thought it was all part of the show.

"Wait till you see this, guys!"

The DJs' equipment went silent and the men in coveralls were back, taking the equipment off the stage. Team Klaus was already gone. Barton didn't notice. He tightened both his grip on the maid and on the clock and took a huge swing with the clock.

Chris said, "Aren't you supposed to be, like, blindfolded or something?"

The clock smacked into the maid's meaty hip. Barton continued to bash the clock into the piñata until it started to tear.

A burst of sunlight came out, illuminating the porch and everyone else gathered around. Barton kept hitting the piñata until a few pieces of candy dropped onto the patio with a wettish plop.

"Oh, hey, candy," Chris said. He bent down to grab it and Barton brought the clock down on the back of his head. A beam of sunlight shot up into the air and Barton raised his head to look at it, hoping to see it streak across the sky. The only things he saw were the space birds. Still circling. Lower now.

Polly screamed and turned to run off. She was drunk and fat so she nearly face planted when she fell down. Barton dragged the maid over to Polly.

"Don't!" the maid shouted.

Barton shook her and said, "I'll fucking do what I want." He threw the clock at Polly. It hit her in the head but not hard enough to make any sunlight come out and probably not hard enough to kill her.

Barton heard the birds in the air and he could see their glistening undersides, lit from the sunlight he'd spilled over the porch.

He could feel the rats under the ground. If he were inside and surrounded by pipes, he would have probably heard them, as well.

Now that he had a free hand he turned to the maid and tore at the buttons of her uniform. She tried to claw his face and he had to tell her it was pointless. There wasn't any sunlight in there. And the look in her eyes was one he couldn't immediately place. He didn't know if he'd ever seen anything quite like it before. He mumbled that he wished there was music and wasn't everything beautiful, all the sunlight.

And then there was even more sunlight.

Coming from his house.

A radiant ball of light, climbing toward the sky, lifting the birds.

The birds crested higher into the sky, en masse, and then came shooting toward him.

He screamed.

20.

The music ending was like throwing back the curtain on an aural horror show. Of course, Alex thought, the music would have gone with the rest of the electricity. He ran toward the sound of the screaming and the sadistic laughter. He heard a *whoosh* and turned to see the house he was just in go up in flames.

What the fuck?

"Ibbie!" he shouted.

He no longer had any idea what was going on. The money was now the furthest thing from his mind. He just wanted to find Ibbie and get the fuck out of here.

21.

Barton didn't want to let go of the maid but he couldn't take his eyes off the birds racing toward him, black against the hell orange of his burning house.

He decided to use the maid as a shield. He yanked her in front of him and said, "Do you see them?"

"Please let me go. I think we need to get out of here."

"Then you see them?"

"Yes. They're coming right for us."

"What are they carrying in their beaks? Can you see that?"

"I don't ..."

"You don't see anything! You're a fucking rat!"

Barton was again conscious of his engorged penis pressing against the maid's ass. He finished shucking off her one-piece uniform skirt until she was in front of him, her back to him, in nothing but her bra, underwear, and tennis shoes. He forced her to the brick of the patio and crushed his hips against her ass, grabbed her by the ponytail and yanked her head up.

"I'm going to fuck you just like I did your mother."

"That was my aunt." The stupid bitch was crying. He didn't see why she had to disagree with him. He was paying her. He was paying everybody. He was paying everybody to make his life the most exciting life ever. And he wanted to think he'd fucked this girl's mom yesterday and was fucking her today. He didn't know why but that thought made him feel good inside. Made him feel warm. And she had to ruin it. In the immediate distance, he saw that dog again. It looked like it was carrying a hand in its mouth.

"Oh, fuck, why don't you just go away and leave me alone."

Behind the dog, Barton thought he saw a man running toward them. He thought the man looked a lot like him. Same wig. Same glasses. Same shorts. Good taste.

22.

On the way to the main house, Alex didn't bother sticking to the out of the way paths. He walked across the expansive lawn he'd spent so much time maintaining. The blaze behind him cast an amazing amount of light over the yard. There were a number of holes dug up throughout the lawn and a lot of bones scattered about. He was pretty sure there was a dog in front of him but he wouldn't really swear to anything at this point. As he drew closer to the main house he tried to focus on the patio. That was mostly out of the perimeter of the fire behind him and it was too dark to make anything out. He still heard the screaming and the laughter and he knew Ibbie was over there. His bad feeling grew increasingly dark.

Then that house burst into flame also.

He ran harder, careful not to hit any of the holes that had been dug up.

23.

The bitch was struggling too much for him to do anything he wanted to do so he decided to kill her so he could drag her body somewhere with less going on and have his way with it. Maybe make another piñata. No. That was a stupid idea. Mexico Frat Funland had been a complete disaster. He'd never try to do that again.

The main house burst into flames and Barton's first thought was that his mom and dad were going to be really mad. Then he remembered he didn't have to worry about them anymore.

He wrapped his hands around the maid's neck.

She squirmed violently beneath him and he looked away from the house and down at her. He wanted to see her muscles all tensed up and writhing beneath her tan skin. Not that he could be any more turned on than he already was but he thought it would be an image he could file away. Maybe use for jerk off material at some later date.

The maid was gone.

He was humping and choking a mass of rats.

They must have come from the house.

Sure. The fire probably drove them out.

But what had happened to the maid?

She was so pretty. So much younger than that other one.

His erection still didn't go away. It may have been medically impossible for it to go away. But the sexual desire he'd felt was replaced with an intense rage. He squeezed even harder. Some kind of grunting sound was coming from his mouth and he didn't mind.

There was a shriek from overhead and he craned his neck to look at all the space birds swooping toward him. He concentrated on the one closest to him. It was gliding toward his face. He tried to make out the thing dangling from its beak, the same thing that dangled from the rest of the birds' beaks. He thought it was a heart.

The bird hit him in the face, knocking him off the mass of wriggling rats.

The sky glowed orange around him and he imagined the blood of a hundred thousand people illuminating the sky.

24.

Alex could make out the scene on the porch. It was King, crouched on Ibbie. It had to be Ibbie. Alex didn't think of what he would do to King when he caught him. He just wanted to get him off Ibbie. Get Ibbie out of here.

Before he reached them, he saw King reel back and land on his back like he was having some kind of fit. Since he was temporarily out of the way, Alex went immediately to Ibbie.

He squatted down next to her. Her eyes were closed. He couldn't tell if she was breathing or not. The air was filled with choking smoke and it was intensely hot. Alex wondered if he should do anything about King or not. He didn't seem to have a gun or any type of weapon so he didn't seem to pose an immediate threat.

Alex scooped Ibbie up, his main desire to get away from the fire and down to the road. He really hoped Joe would be waiting for them. The last thing he wanted was to be caught on this property after all this shit had gone down.

He whispered into Ibbie's ear, "Baby. Baby, are you

okay?"

There wasn't any response and he wasn't sure he expected one.

He heard squealing brakes and looked over toward the driveway.

It was his car with, presumably, Joe behind the wheel. It was screeching to a stop because there was a man standing in the driveway carrying a suitcase.

The car didn't stop fast enough. It hit the man. He didn't go up on the hood like pedestrians do in movies. He was dragged under the car and the car finally came to a stop somewhere over him. The suitcase he'd been holding exploded. Cash went everywhere. The suitcase, still half full, continued to roll along the driveway.

Joe got out of the car and started grabbing for the cash.

Alex didn't know what Joe was thinking.

"Joe! Don't touch it!"

"What?"

"Just leave it!"

"But ..."

"Yeah, I know. Just leave it."

Alex was now at the car. He decided Joe wouldn't be fast enough so he put Ibbie in the back seat and told Joe to take shotgun. He turned around in the driveway, mangled the yard, and put the two flaming houses and all the other crazy shit behind them. For once, he was glad the hospital was on the good side of town.

25.

Barton lay on his back while the birds gathered around him. They were all over him, preventing him from moving his arms or his legs. The largest one hopped onto his chest. It was so large he could actually feel it pressing down on his chest. He thought birds were supposed to be light. *Light as a bird.* Wasn't that a popular expression? Or was it light as a feather? He was still conscious of his penis pressing against his shorts, almost painfully. The bird started pecking on his chest. He noticed it was the only one he'd seen that didn't have a heart dangling from its beak and became suddenly aware of what it was trying to do.

He screamed and thrashed but it didn't do any good.

The bird continued to peck until its beak finally tore through his shirt and then he could feel it breaking through his skin and he thought maybe this was what he wanted anyway. No. He was pretty sure that was stupid. He was pretty sure people couldn't live without hearts. Unless the magic space birds knew something he didn't. Maybe they replaced the heart with something else. Something even better. Like maybe a space heart. Barton continued to watch, hoping he was filled with sunshine just like everyone else. But he didn't see any sunshine pouring out of his wound. Two of the birds plucked out his eyes and everything went black as he felt the large bird sink its head into his chest cavity and pull his heart out.

Barton thought the absence of a heart would have killed him but it seemed to only heighten his senses. Except for his sense of sight, because he no longer had any eyes. But he didn't really need them. He'd seen this estate so much over the years it was burned into his mind. And the current vision of it in his head was one of sheer beauty. Houses burning. Dead bodies everywhere. The lawn dug up. Sirens in the distance. And something else.

William.

He could sense William.

He wasn't that far away.

Barton didn't quite think he could stand to walk so he crawled. He could feel something leaking from his empty eye sockets and hoped it was sunshine.

It didn't take him as long as he thought it would to reach William.

William wasn't moving.

"William?" Barton said.

William didn't answer him.

Barton pressed his mouth to William's. He tasted blood and something even worse. Disease or shit or something. Maybe William ate his own shit. Maybe he ate other people's. Barton had heard of people doing that. He stuck his tongue into William's mouth. Again, Barton's attention was drawn to his throbbing penis.

"William, buddy, I'm gonna put my dick in your mouth. Is that okay?"

William didn't answer.

The sirens drew closer.

Barton rose to his knees and unzipped his shorts. The warm night air felt great on his penis. He crawled on top of William and tried to guide his penis into the man's mouth.

Barton heard voices.

"Groundskeeper said not to worry, he was just burning off some shrubs."

"Jesus. What the fuck?"

"Hey, look over there."

Barton found William's mouth and began thrusting into it. He wished he had like six dicks to put in there. And he wished William's mouth was filled with snakes or maybe a bunch of those little lizards. Barton continued to thrust faster. He could see the sunlight on the horizon. It had already circled the earth and come back again. He wondered how he could see it without any eyes and realized it was inside of him. It always was. And then he saw the space birds quickly disappear through a hole in the sky, hiding from the sunlight, hiding from the sunshine exploding inside Barton. Exploding out of Barton and into William's mouth and everything went silent and calm and warm.

26.

Joe wouldn't shut up. The cheap car was loud enough as it was and Alex was trying to listen for any sound of Ibbie taking a breath. He could have told Joe to monitor if the guy would shut up long enough for Alex to tell him. Alex should have made Joe drive so he could sit with Ibbie, at least to confirm if she were alive or dead. He didn't know what else he could do.

"I think I killed that guy. I think I killed that guy. I think I killed that guy. I think I killed that guy."

Alex reached over and punched Joe hard on the thigh. "Shut the fuck up!"

Alex had just thought of something and it wasn't good. If they took Ibbie to the hospital for smoke inhalation or strangulation and paramedics and ambulances had undoubtedly been dispatched to the King house, it was going to be extremely suspicious. He might as well just drive them to the jail. If it meant Ibbie were going to live, he would gladly do it. But if she were already dead or if her vitals seemed okay, there wasn't any need to go to the hospital.

They were already at the hospital.

He pulled into the parking lot rather than drive up to the front door.

"What are we doing?" Joe asked.

"I'll explain later."

"I think I killed that guy back there."

Alex raised his fist and Joe shut up. Alex got out of the car and opened the back door.

He hadn't realized how bad Ibbie had been. Her neck was swollen. Her eyes were open and rolled back in her head. He didn't need to feel for a pulse or press his cheek against her mouth to feel for breath but he did. He bypassed tears and went immediately into shock.

Joe had opened the other door and had his head leaned over Ibbie. "Why's she holding those, Alex? What happened to Ibbie, Alex? What the fuck is going on?" Joe was crying, almost blubbering. "What the fuck is going on, Alex?"

Alex didn't answer him. He didn't see any point in answering him. Didn't see any point in anything at the moment. He looked at Ibbie's hands to see what she was holding. Her left hand clutched a rat and her right hand clutched a bird. Alex backed out of the car and shut the door.

He looked toward the King estate, the orange glow painting the sky. He began walking in the opposite direction. He could hear Joe blubbering and it seemed so far away. He heard Joe get back into the car and start it up. Alex found that he wanted Joe to drive the car into him, from behind, so he didn't know it was happening until he felt the impact. But he heard the car moving in the opposite direction and Alex turned to see where he was going and watched Joe pull the car onto the main road and drive into the night.

Other Grindhouse Press Titles

#666 – *Satanic Summer*
by Andersen Prunty

#014 – *How To Kill Yourself*
by C.V. Hunt

#013 – *Bury the Children in the Yard: Horror Stories*
by Andersen Prunty

#012 – *Return to Devil Town (Vampires in Devil Town Book Three)*
by Wayne Hixon

#011 – *Pray You Die Alone: Horror Stories*
by Andersen Prunty

#010 – *King of the Perverts*
by Steve Lowe

#009 – *Sunruined: Horror Stories*
by Andersen Prunty